SCHOOL MEMORIES

Story and Art by

Sharean Morishita

Proofread/ Rebecca Scoble
Beta Reader/ Mika, Cassandra & Diana Farmer
Editor/ Brian Denham

THIS MAY SOUND WEIRD BUT...

I THINK THIS SCHOOL YEAR'S REALLY GONNA STINK.

AND IT'S ALL BECAUSE OF HER.

THE GIRL WHO RUINED MY SCHOOL LIFE.

SPLASH
I LIKE PULLING HARMLESS PRANKS SOMETIMES.
PFFFT!
GETTING OTHER'S TO LAUGH MAKES ME FEEL LIKE I FIT IN.
TMP
TMP
TMP
HA
HA HA HA
BUT NOT EVERYONE UNDERSTANDS THAT, AND SOMETIMES THEY BLOW THINGS WAY OUT OF PROPORTION.
COLTON WHY CAN'T YOU SEE HOW MEAN THESE PRANKS ARE?!
AWW C'MON, IT'S FUNNY!
NO, IT'S ONLY FUNNY TO YOU BECAUSE YOU'VE NEVER ENDURED OUR STRUGGLE FIRSTHAND.
Apologize!
Apologize!
Apologize!
Apologize!
Apologize!
DWOOooo
ULP
IT-WAS-A-JOKE!
OKAY, SURE I'M IN THE WRONG FOR MAKING HER CRY, BUT...

YOU CAN EITHER FIND A PARTNER TO DO THE NOW-MANDATORY EXTRA CREDIT HAIR ASSIGNMENT...
OR WE CAN SEE WHAT YOUR PARENTS HAVE TO SAY ABOUT THIS.
DoooOm
UH... MRS. DAYE? ISN'T THAT JUST FOR HALF-SEMESTER STUDENTS? HE'S THE ONLY ONE...
JUSTICE PREVAILS!
HUH ?!
EVERYTHING WAS GOING GREAT, UNTIL...
E-excuse me... Mrs. Daye?
Hmm?
WOO HOO
YOU'RE RIGHT, COLTON. JUSTICE TRULY HAS PREVAILED.
HELLO MY NAME IS ECHO AND I'M HERE FOR THE HALF SEMESTER CLASS CREDIT.

YOU'LL BE DOING EACH OTHER'S HAIR FOR THIS ASSIGNMENT.
THIS IS PERFECT TIMING SINCE SCHOOL PICTURE DAY IS COMING UP!
MY MOM SAYS I'M NOT ALLOWED TO DO HAIR.
HUH?
I TRIED DOING ISABELLA'S HAIR, BUT LOOK WHAT HAPPENED.
I'LL DO ANYTHING BUT THAT!!
CENSORED
IT'S OKAY, BELLA, I STILL LOVE YOU.
HOW IS THAT EVEN POSSIBLE?!
NO WORRIES, THIS LESSON GUIDE SHOULD COME IN HANDY.

NO! I'M FIGHTING THIS! I DID NOTHING WRONG!
ARE YOU TWO RAISING YOUR VOICES AT ME?
B-BUT I DON'T KNOW HOW TO DO HAIR!
GONE ARE THE DAYS WHEN WE ALL GOT ALONG AND JUST LAUGHED AT JOKES!
I CAN'T DO STUFF I DON'T KNOW HOW TO DO! I NEED MORE TIME!
KRRK
N-NO MA'AM! JUST A YOUTHFUL INDISCRETION.
GONG
...
WHINE
WHINE
GOOD. NOW YOU'RE EITHER DOING THE ASSIGNMENT OR I'M TELLING BOTH OF YOUR PARENTS ABOUT YOUR BEHAVIOR!
WHICH WILL IT BE?
THE ASSIGNMENT PLEASE.

I SERIOUSLY HAVE THE WORST LUCK EVER.

YOUR HAIR'S NOT SUPPOSED TO SMELL LIKE THIS, RIGHT?

DID I USE THE WRONG PRODUCT?

UH OH! IT'S MATTING UP YOUR HAIR NOW! ISN'T THIS A DETANGLER?!

SHE'S BEEN AT THIS FOR OVER AN HOUR!

CENSORED

MY BEHIND HAS GONE NUMB FROM SITTING ON THIS HARD FLOOR.

CENSORED

UH... EXCUSE ME, BUT IS THERE A TANGLE TEASER IN OUR BOX?

OR MAYBE A DENIM BRUSH? I WANT TO GET THESE TANGLES OUT WITH AS LITTLE PAIN AS POSSIBLE.
CENSORED
WHO CARES. JUST USE A WIDE TOOTH COMB OR WHATEVER. I DON'T SEE THE BIG DEAL.

BUT ALL THE WIDE TOOTH COMBS ARE MISSING.
THEY AREN'T MISSING, THE OTHER KIDS HID THEM TO BE FUNNY.
HERE, USE THIS COMB INSTEAD.

TH-THAT'S A RAT TAIL COMB!
ARE YOU CRAZY?!
A COMB IS A COMB AND BOTH OF MY BUTT CHEEKS HAVE GONE COLD SO JUST USE IT!

O-OKAY... H-HERE I GO.
B-BMP
B-BMP
B-BMP
B-BMP
B-BMP
YANK
I... I GOT THE FIRST TANGLE OUT.
? ? ?
MRS. DAYE! I'VE KILLED HIM!!

I'VE NEVER KNOWN A PAIN LIKE THAT EXISTED BEFORE ...

NO ONE COULD POSSIBLY BE THAT BAD AT DOING HAIR.

MAYBE THIS WAS HER BAD ATTEMPT AT A PRANK?

PRANKS ARE SUPPOSED TO BE FUNNY NOT PAINFUL.

I NEED TO SHOW HER HOW TO PULL A GOOD PRANK THAT'S ACTUALLY FUNNY OR SHE'LL NEVER MAKE FRIENDS.

I ALSO CAN'T HAVE MY ASSIGNMENT PARTNER BEING THIS TERRIBLE AT PRANKS.

It's my pride as a class clown

I'VE SEEN PLENTY OF FUNNY HAIR PRANK VIDEOS...
THEY'VE GONE VIRAL ONLINE, SO I'M SURE EVERYONE HERE WILL LOVE THEM, TOO.
Oh no! My hair is falling out!
Gotcha! That wasn't your hair!
You're so clever, cool and EXTREMLY handsome!
I was so wrong this is funny!
We now have a sense of humor thanks to you!
HEH-HEH... THAT'S PERFECT! ABSOLUTELY FOOLPROOF!
UM, MRS. DAYE WANT'S US TO PICK A SINK STATION TO DO THE WASH-AND-GOS.
THEY'LL ALL BE LIKE "COLTON YOU'RE SO AWESOME LET'S BE FRIENDS!" HEH-HEH!
I-I'M READY FOR YOU TO WASH MY HAIR NOW.
Excuse me? Hello~o?
I'LL JUST MIX SOME OF THIS IN WITH HER HAIR.
I'll get the clarifying shampoo
CUBAN TWIST
THEN I'LL PRETEND LIKE I USED THE WRONG PRODUCT AND IT'S MAKING HER HAIR FALL OUT.

HEY, UM, DON'T PANIC BUT I THINK I USED THE WRONG PRODUCT.
W-WRONG PRODUCT?
I DON'T KNOW, JUST A LOT OF HAIR IS FALLING OUT AND I-
I'M SORRY! I CAN'T GET IT TO STOP COMING OUT!
M-MY HAIR?!
N-NO! MY HAIR! IT WON'T STOP!!
KA-TUNK
SMP

WAIT! CALM DOWN! IT'S A PRANK.
WH-WHAT?
IT'S A JOKE. SEE? IT'S NOT YOUR REAL HAIR, IT'S JUST SOME BRAIDING WEAVE.
ARE YOU SERIOUS?! HAHAHA! GOOD ONE, COLTON!
...
DID YOU HEAR HOW LOUD SHE WAS SCREAMING?!
THAT'S SO FUNNY!! DID YOU SEE HOW SHE FELL?!
THAT'S SO LAME! ANYONE COULD'VE SEEN HOW FAKE IT WAS! HAHAHA!
I KNEW IT WOULD BE A BIG HIT! EVERYONE LOVES IT!

HEY COLTON, TELL THE NEW GIRL TO LIGHTEN UP!
COME ON NEW GIRL, IT'S JUST A JOKE! LAUGH!
...
JUST IGNORE HER, COLTON. SHE JUST DOESN'T HAVE A SENSE OF HUMOR.
BYE, YOU KILLJOY! HA-HA-HA!
....WHY ISN'T SHE LAUGHING WITH US?
I DIDN'T MEAN ANYTHING BY IT....
KR\\\
KR\\\
KR\\\
KR\\\
IT'S JUST A FUNNY JOKE...

SINCE THEN SHE STARTED WORKING ON MOST OF THE ASSIGNMENT WITHOUT ME.
I TRIED INVITING HER TO EAT LUNCH WITH THE REST OF OUR CLASS SO WE COULD GET TO KNOW EACH OTHER...
BUT WHENEVER I TRY TALKING TO HER SHE ALWAYS RUNS AWAY FROM ME.
I WANTED HER TO SEE THAT I'M NOT A BAD PERSON.
I DON'T GET IT...
WHY IS SHE AVOIDING ME?

HEY UH-...
N-NEW GIRL?
CAN I TALK
TO YOU FOR
A SECOND?

JEEZ!
I REALLY
SHOULD'VE
AT LEAST
LEARNED

OKAY...
WHAT
DO YOU
WANT?
LOOK...
I DON'T
KNOW IF
IT'S JUST
ME, BUT...

IT FEELS
LIKE YOU'RE
UPSET
WITH ME.

I
THINK MAYBE
YOU MIGHT HAVE
MISUNDERSTOOD...
I
DIDN'T MEAN
ANYTHING
BY THE PRANK
I WAS JUST
POKING FUN.
...

WELL...

I'VE ALWAYS GOT PICKED ON OR POKED AT FOR FUN AT EVERY NEW SCHOOL I'VE ATTENDED....

MY MOM'S JOB HAS US MOVING A LOT SO I'VE NEVER HAD A CHANCE TO FIT IN....
SINCE YOU WERE THE FIRST PERSON TO ACTUALLY TALK TO ME I THOUGHT THIS TIME WOULD BE DIFFERENT
THAT MAYBE I WOULDN'T FEEL LIKE AN OUTSIDER ANYMORE....

IF YOU WERE IN MY SHOES HOW WOULD YOU FEEL AFTER ALL OF THIS?
...

I SHOULD GO NOW...
W-WAIT! NEW-UH-I-I MEAN ...UM WHAT'S YOUR NAME?...
IT'S ECHO.
TODAY'S THE LAST DAY TO FINISH THE ASSIGNMENT FOR PICTURE DAY....
YOU HAVEN'T FINISHED YOUR HALF RIGHT?
WE CAN FINISH IT FASTER IF WE WORK TOGETHER...
OKÄY.
T-thank you
A-ARE YOU SURE THIS IS GOING TO DRY IN TIME?
YES! MY MOM SWEARS BY THIS SETTING LOTION!
NOW, TELL ME AGAIN WHY YOU PICKED THIS HAIRSTYLE INSTEAD OF THE WASH-AND-GO FOR THE END PRODUCT?
CAUSE IT'S THE SAME HAIRSTYLE MY MOM WORE FOR HER SCHOOL PICTURE DAY!

SEE, YOUR HAIRS ALL DRY~ I TOLD YA. THAT STUFF IS GOOD OL' FAITHFUL.
IT WAS REALLY NICE OF YOU TO HELP ME FINISH IN TIME!
DOES THIS MEAN THAT YOU DON'T THINK I'M SUCH A BAD GUY, RIGHT?
I DIDN'T THINK *YOU* WERE BAD IT WAS YOUR *PRANKS*.
...
Direct
THEN WHY WERE YOU ALWAYS RUNNING AWAY FROM ME?
BECAUSE I THOUGHT YOU WERE TRYING TO PULL ANOTHER PRANK ON ME.
....

Chit-Chat Corner

I used to go to this certain school back when I was 14, and since I showed up during the middle of the third semester, everyone already knew each other and so I was named the "New Girl"

Even after the next school year started, I was still called the new girl.

I remember one humiliating time during gym class when we had to play soccer. I was on the defense team so when I saw this boy rampaging towards me with the ball I froze, and he kicked the ball right in my gut. I fell to the ground like a sack of rocks.

The whole team comes running towards me screeching "Look what you did to the New Girl!" and while I laid curled on the dirt utterly embarrassed, all I could really think was, "I've been here a whole year. Why don't they know my name?"

I CAN'T BELIEVE I GET TO PARTICIPATE IN SCHOOL PICTURE DAY

I COULD NEVER GET THIS HAIRSTYLE RIGHT ON MY OWN.

SO YOU'VE NEVER STAYED LONG ENOUGH AT A SCHOOL TO TAKE PICTURES?

YEAH.... MY MOM REALLY BEATS HERSELF UP ABOUT IT TOO...

SHE SAYS SHES THE REASON I DON'T HAVE A LOT OF SCHOOL MEMORIES

Look that's The girl from class!

Shh! I have a real funny idea!

SHE'S REALLY NICE....
SO I WANTED TO TAKE THESE SCHOOL PICTURES SO SHE DOESN'T HAVE TO FEEL BAD.
THAT WAY SHE CAN SEE THAT I STILL MADE SOME SCHOOL MEMORIES!
HAD I REALIZED HOW NICE OF A PERSON SHE WAS I NEVER WOULD HAVE....
...EITHER WAY ....WHAT I DID STILL WASN'T COOL...

BUT PULLING PRANKS IS THE ONLY WAY PEOPLE WILL LIKE ME....
THERE'S NOTHING ELSE FUN ABOUT ME...
IT'S FUN JUST TALKING TO ME?
COLTON, THANK YOU AGAIN FOR HELPING ME AND FOR TALKING TO ME.
YOU HELPED MAKE THIS THE BEST DAY EVER!
TALKING TO YOU WAS THE MOST FUN I'VE EVER HAD AT ANY SCHOOL!

HEY NEW GIRL?
HEADS UP!
SPL—ASH

Chill! It's a joke!
What the heck is your problem?!
Ha-ha-ha! Look at her face!
Hey... umm -sniff- c-can you do me a favor?
Come on, let's go before the teacher shows up!
But those guys just-
It's okay...
Can you go get a teacher?
Please.

ALRIGHT...
I'LL BE
RIGHT BACK.

TODAY'S
THE LAST DAY
FOR SCHOOL
PICTURES...

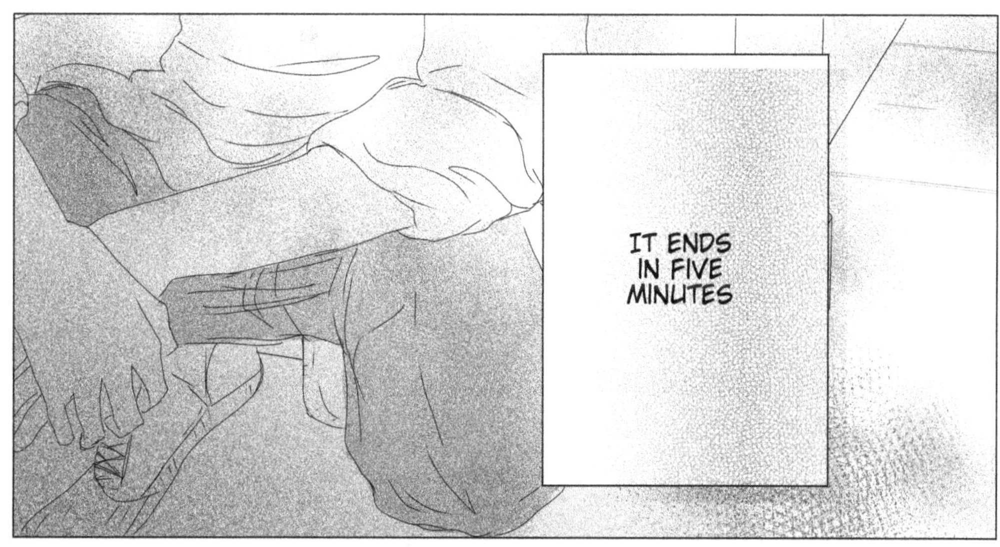

IT ENDS
IN FIVE
MINUTES

SHE'LL
NEVER BE
ABLE TO REDO
EVERYTHING
AND MAKE IT
IN TIME.

HEY COLTON! NO HARD FEELINGS ABOUT YESTERDAY, RIGHT?
SURE, MAN! NO HARM, NO FOUL, RIGHT?
BY THE WAY, YOU GUYS SHOULD TRY THIS NEW HAIR PRODUCT!
I HEARD IT'S FIRE!
sure! bring it!
He said scrub your scalp with your nails.
The tingling means it's working.
LYE HAIR MAS
MY HEAD IS ON FIRE!
Stop being dramatic.
Chill out. It's just a hair mask.
COLTON, GET BACK HERE!
ECHO STOPPED COMING TO CLASS AFTER THAT DAY...

IT PROBABLY WOULD HAVE BEEN BETTER IF WE NEVER MET...
HEY MR. CLARK, LONG TIME NO SEE!
COLTON.
THAT WAY SHE WOULDN'T HAVE GOTTEN PICKED ON....
MR. CLARK? SORRY I'M A LITTLE LATE.
NO WORRIES, COME ON IN!
OUR SCHOOL'S BIG, SO IT ALWAYS TAKES NEW STUDENTS A WHILE TO GET USED TO IT.
GO AHEAD AND PICK ANY EMPTY SEAT.

AND I WOULDN'T HAVE REALIZE THAT I'M MISSING OUT ON MAKING AN AWESOME FRIEND....

THIS SCHOOL YEAR WAS REALLY GOING TO SUCK...

AND IT'S ALL BECAUSE OF THIS GIRL...

THANK YOU FOR READING!

I wanted to do this short story as a personal challenge
to work on my storytelling. For these particular characters
I wanted to do their story for many years now. I keep the ending
an open ending so that if my creative battery recharges
I can always come back and continue this story.

I do hope you all enjoyed reading this comic as much as I enjoy making it!

Thank you again for reading!
Sharean Morishita

Random comic clip
↓ Anyone else remember the pain of that
rat tale comb ripping through your hair?

SPECIAL THANK YOU PAGE:

It's because of these dear readers and supporters
that I was able to make this book a reality!

2022 Patreon Supporters:

https://www.patreon.com/smorishita

Kammy
Halle Nelson
Dylan Williams
Kakusagi カクサギ
Rainy Fristoe
H.
Yogo Sapphirey
Keke Banks
H
Lady Ashuri
Arj
Jasmine Saunders
Perlenoire77Chan
Faye Singleton
Leah Fields-Nester
Royce Adkins
Duokhay
Epiphany Gross-Gaynair

夢子
Warrior_princess
Adina Taylor
Diamond Wilson
Giselle Leung
Kym
Soprano Musings
Kevin Kubli
Marwa Al-Alawi
Geneva Bowers
Birdie
Jun♥Chu
Mary Owolabi
Christine Brunson
Jay Lofstead
N'jaila Rhee
MS.Pol
Whitney Dyer

Erica L
Naomie
Cassia Clark
Joleen White
Michelle Scott
Prettyism
Little_me
Ambyr

Thank you so much for all of your support cheering me on while I learn how to make comics and tell fun stories~